THE END OF THE WORLD

by Henriette Major

Illustrated by Philippe Béha

Translated from the French by Alan Brown

Le bout du monde
Original edition
© Les Éditions Héritage Inc. 1987

The End of the World
Translation by Alan Brown
Copyright © by McClelland and Stewart, 1988

This translation was completed with the assistance
of the Canada Council.

Canadian Cataloguing in Publication Data

Major, Henriette, 1933–
    [Le bout du monde. English]
    The end of the world

Translation of: Le bout du monde.
ISBN 0–7710–5472–6

I. Béha, Philippe. II. Title. III. Title:
Le bout du monde. English.

PS8576.A52B6913 1988   jC843'.54   C88–094352–1
PZ7.M335En 1988

Typeset by VictoR GAD studio
Printed and bound in Canada

McClelland and Stewart
The Canadian Publishers
481 University Avenue
Toronto, Ontario
M5G 2E9

Near a shimmering pond there lived two wild ducks: a young lady duck and a drake (that's what we call a male duck). They had only hatched a few months before, so they hadn't seen much of the world.

One day the drake said to his young wife, "Come with me, I'll take you to the end of the world."

She agreed and became very excited because that sounded like a wonderful place to go. So they started their voyage, swimming across the shimmering pond. When they reached the other side, the drake said proudly, "Here we are! This is the end of the world!"

"That's not the end of the world," said the duck. "It's only the end of the pond."

"Well, it's the end of the world for me," said the drake. "It's the end of my world."

"You can't see past the end of your beak!" the duck exclaimed. "If that's the way it is, you can stay in your shimmering pond. I'm going to look for the end of the world."

And away she went. Behind the pond there was a dark forest. The duck was no sooner under the leafy trees than she saw a squirrel.

"Squirrel," she said, "how do I get to the end of the world?"

"The end of the world?" said the squirrel, cocking his head on one side. "Let's see now, I think it's that way. Come on, follow me."

The squirrel, feeling very important, led her to the other side of the forest. There he stopped and refused to go any farther.

The duck was very disappointed. She saw that for the squirrel the end of the world was the end of the woods. She thanked him for his help, but she was determined to go farther because she could see that the world went on and on.

When she left the forest behind, she saw a very different world. In the distance there were fences, houses, fields of grain. In the meadow that skirted the woods a big animal was eating grass. The duck waddled closer to it.

"Excuse me," she said, "is this the way to the end of the world?"

"I don't know, and I don't want to know," said the cow. "Would you like some grass?"

"No, thanks," said the duck. "By the way, you're not very curious, are you? Don't you care about the end of the world?"

"That depends. Have they got better grass at the end of the world?"

"I don't know. I've never been there."

"Well, what interests me," said the cow, "is good, green grass. And that's what I have here."

"What interests me," said the duck, "is seeing the end of the world."

And she waddled away. Now, ducks and drakes are not very good walkers. They usually like to swim or fly. So the duck flew off over the field. Everything she saw from up there surprised her, for she had never been away from her pond before. Far away she saw a road, but she took it for a river. She dived down to have a little paddle in the water.

"My word!" she quacked as she landed. "This must be a river of stones!"

Just then a truck came along. The duck was terrified. She hid in the ditch. But the farmer, who was driving the truck, had caught a glimpse of the poor bird. He stopped and got out to take a closer look at this surprising sight.

"Good day to you," he said. "What are you doing here?"

"Good day to you too," the duck replied. She had the shivers in her voice. (It was the first time she'd seen such a big, two-legged creature.) "Can you tell me where the end of the world is?"

"Why, that's easy," the farmer replied. "Get into my truck, I'll take you there."

And the farmer made a comfortable seat for the duck on an orange crate beside him, so that she could see the fields go by.

"My, I'm lucky," the duck said to herself. "It's a good thing I left my shimmering pond. Here I am being driven to the end of the world on a river of stones in a rolling nest, with a two-legged beast! My husband, the drake, will never believe me when I tell him about this."

At last they arrived at the farm. Suddenly the farmer caught the duck and locked her up in the chicken house with five hens and a shabby-looking old rooster. Then the farmer left, very pleased with himself.

A little giddy from her trip, the duck shook herself to wake up.

"What kind of an impolite creature is this?" the shabby rooster cried in an unfriendly voice. "What are you doing here?"

"To tell you the truth, I don't know. You see, I'm on a trip to the end of the world, but I met a two-legged animal who shut me up in this dirty place. There must be some mistake."

At these words all the hens started clucking together.

"Really, the nerve! . . . "

"Who does she think she is?"

"Did you ever see the like?"

But the rooster had the last word.

"You can put on airs all you like, young lady, but you'll end up in the cooking pot just like the rest of us. That's the end of the world for creatures like you and me."

The duck didn't know what a cooking pot was, but it sounded scary. So, when the farmer's wife came in to feed the hens, the duck slipped between her legs, spread her wings and flew off. She was far away before anyone could run after her.

High in the air the duck saw a seagull doing some stunt flying.
That looks like fun! she thought.
And she began to try some of the seagull's tricks, a loop-the-loop and a dive. She didn't know that you have to practise these tricks for a long time.

Ducks are not very good at stunt flying. She had only tried one loop when she tumbled right into a straw stack. She had no broken bones, but her feathers were badly ruffled. The seagull, which had been watching her, at once flew down to see if she was hurt.

"You act pretty funny for a duck," the gull said, "but you look like a nice kid. Can I help you in any way?"

"Well, yes," said the duck, who never missed a chance. "Maybe you can tell me something: I'm looking for the end of the world."

"The end of the world?" the seagull repeated very seriously. "In a way it's right here. Just imagine that the world is a balloon. If you fly right around it, you always come back to where you started."

"That's no fun," said the duck. "I might as well give up right away."

"No, no," said the gull. "Don't be discouraged. If you like, I'll take you to see a friend of mine. He's a very wise old owl, and he may know more than we do."

Soon they were at the foot of the hollow tree where the old owl lived. They had to wake him up because owls sleep in the daytime and go hunting at night. But the old owl didn't mind, and was actually very flattered at being asked hard questions.

"Hum, hum!" he said when he had heard their story. "You're looking for the end of the world? Well, I'll tell you how to find it."

"Oh, yes, please do!" cried the duck, all excited.

"Just stay still," the owl commanded, "and shut your eyes."

And the owl began to sing very softly. Not knowing what was happening, the duck and the seagull felt their eyes getting tired. They were almost sleeping, almost dreaming.

"That's your answer," the owl whispered softly in their ears. "Now you know how to find the end of the world."

And he drew back into his hole in the tree. After a moment the seagull opened her eyes.

"Now I understand," she said. "The end of the world is inside us. We can go there in our dreams."

But the duck was not so sure.

"You mean I can get to the world's end just by dreaming? I don't believe it. I'm going to go on looking for the end of the world. Maybe it's that way . . . "

And away she waddled, and away she flew, straight ahead. Last time she was heard of she was still looking for the end of the world . . . on the Island of Madagascar!

THE END